My Baby & Me

concept and words by
Lynn Reiser

photographs by
Penny Gentieu

Alfred A. Knopf
New York

Hey, little baby!

What can **you** do?

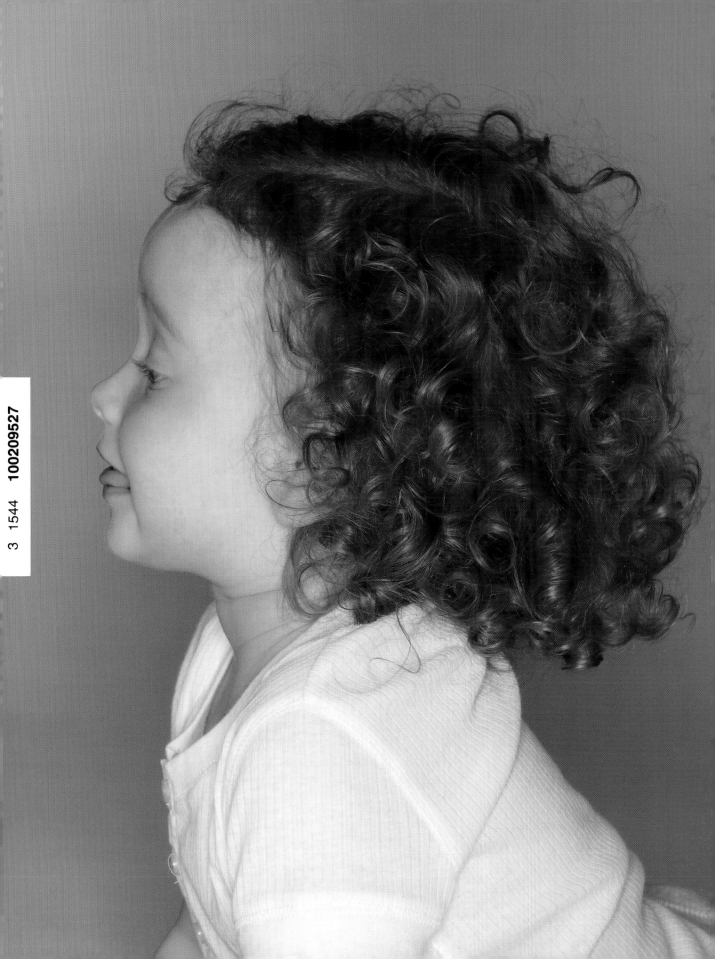

You can smile?

I can too.

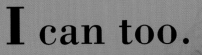

You can crawl?

Watch **me** go.
I go fast—
You go slow!

You can bounce?

I can hop!

I can pick up things you drop.

That's your bunny.
Here's **my** bear.

That's your car seat. Here's **my** chair.

You have a bottle!

I have a cup!
I pour juice in.
I drink it up.

I can read.
Here's **my** book.

I can show you.
Look, look, look!

See **me** build—
Way up high.

I can crash it.
You can try!

Now, little baby!

What can **we** do?

You hug **me**,
and I'll hug **you**!

To John and Suzy. —L. R.

To my brother Peter and sister Sally for their kindness and generosity. —P. G.

THIS IS A BORZOI BOOK PUBLISHED BY ALFRED A. KNOPF

Text copyright © 2008 by Lynn Reiser
Photographs copyright © 2008 by Penny Gentieu

All rights reserved. Published in the United States by Alfred A. Knopf, an imprint of
Random House Children's Books, a division of Random House, Inc., New York.

Knopf, Borzoi Books, and the colophon are registered trademarks of Random House, Inc.

Visit us on the Web! www.randomhouse.com/kids

Educators and librarians, for a variety of teaching tools, visit us at www.randomhouse.com/teachers

Library of Congress Cataloging-in-Publication Data
Reiser, Lynn.
My baby and me / concept and words by Lynn Reiser ; photographs by Penny Gentieu. — 1st ed.
p. cm.
Summary: Photographs and simple text portray interactions between babies and their toddler siblings.
ISBN 978-0-375-85205-3 (trade) — ISBN 978-0-375-95205-0 (lib. bdg.)
[1. Babies—Fiction. 2. Toddlers—Fiction. 3. Brothers and sisters—Fiction. 4. Stories in rhyme.]
I. Gentieu, Penny, ill. II. Title.
PZ8.3.R2757My 2008
[E]—dc22
2007031949

MANUFACTURED IN MALAYSIA
May 2008
10 9 8 7 6 5 4 3 2 1
First Edition

Random House Children's Books supports the First Amendment and celebrates the right to read.